The Terror in WhiteChapel:

What If ?

Wanda May Hawke

Dedication:

This book is dedicated to my Children, Kathryn-Aline (Kate) Alvin-Jay (A.J.) James and My Beautiful Granddaughter Rayna.

You are My heart and the reason I wake up everyday and try to make the world a better Place.

Acknowledgement

I want to thank all the amazing teachers I've was blessed to in my life, to many to mention here but without all of them,

I would have given up on not only school but myself if not for them.

"Dr., what's wrong? This baby is taking so long to come—12 hours for a fifth child?" the midwife was concerned. "I'm glad you are here."

"She needs laudanum. We can work better with her out." The doctor barked.

The baby was born, but the doctor and the midwife were stunned when they looked at the tiny newborn.

He was disfigured. There was a gaping hole where his nose and part of his upper lip should have been. He only had one whole arm, the other with a couple of fingers growing just down from his elbow. The rest was not there.

His chest was barrel-shaped, and his breathing was quite difficult because of it. There were weeping sores over most of his little body; the poor thing was tiny.

"I don't expect this child to last the night," said the doctor, more to himself than anyone in the room.

"Then why shall we even burden the family with him? At all?" the midwife asked.

"What? What's wrong with the baby?" Greta asked weakly from her bed.

The doctor and midwife looked first at the bed and then at each other before the doctor could speak.

"He has difficulties, Mrs. Fallows, and will not live too long."

"Please, please let me see him anyway. Let me wash him and get him comfortable."

The midwife swaddled the baby, trying to hide some of the damage, and handed him to Greta. When she saw his face, she let out a little cry and nearly dropped the baby.

"What is it? What's wrong with him?"

"I don't know, Mrs.," answered the doctor. "But I will do my best to find out."

The boy didn't make it through the night. The doctor asked permission to bring him to the hospital to see why the child was born like this. It may take some time.

Three weeks later, the doctor returned to the house to speak with the Lord and Lady Fallows.

"First, I must say what I found, even I was surprised. Secondly, of course, I am so sorry for your loss. Your son was born with deformities caused by syphilis, which means you, Lady Fallows, were already infected with it before or near conception."

"What? How dare you? I have had but one partner in my life. And he sits here before you."

Greta looked back and forth between the doctor and her husband, and it didn't fall into place immediately. Then, with a shot of anger and clarity, she realised it had to have come from George.

"George, how could you be with another woman? Have I not been a good wife? Have I not given you five, no four beautiful children?"

"That's just it, dear; please calm down. It is a man who has many more needs than his wife. You were pregnant so often and happy with your way of life. I felt lacking and unwanted," replied George.

"So you took a mistress? Do you keep her, too? Do you pay for her food, lodgings, and clothing? Are you taking that money away from your family?"

"Greta, please, calm down; there is no use fighting in front of the doctor; let us discuss this privately."

Greta rang for the butler. "Please show the doctor out, then see that we are not disturbed."

"Here, Greta, have some laudanum the doctor prescribed. It will calm you so we may talk sensibly."

"I don't need to calm myself. I need to understand, George; help me to understand."

"Greta, there is no mistress; I would not disgrace the family like that."

"Then who? Who were you with?" Suddenly, Greta's face changed, first to shock, then to anger. "NO! NO! George, tell me I'm wrong. You were with a common streetwalker, a Dollymop? A... a... 4 penny knee bender?"

"Greta! Please don't let those foul words fall from your mouth."

"Fall from my mouth? Do I offend you? My words and my language offend you!! You slept with those, and my words offend you?"

Taking a moment's breath, Greta continued. "I will not disgrace this household by divorce. We will continue to be Man and Wife, but in name and face only. When in public, you will play the part of a loving husband and me, as hard as it may be, your loving wife. But in this house, we will keep to our rooms; mine, George, will always be off-limits to you. All because you are the one who killed our baby. If you had not been rutting with your pigs, he would not be cold in his grave this night."

London house

Breakfast was always a bustling affair in the Fallows' house; the two older children take it with their parents.

Thomas, the responsible elder brother at twelve; Lydia (Sissy), the budding young lady at ten; Debra (Debbie), the little mother, nine-year-old; and Kevin, the youngest at six, still enjoying the nursery.

Lady Fallows, Greta, was born in Germany, making her different size than most British ladies. At 5'8", she had big bones and large hands.

She preferred reading to the 'ladies' arts of sewing, piano, knitting, etc., as she found solace and knowledge in books. Surprisingly, this led to a rather extensive library built last year, now the Lady's favourite room full of light, books, and plants.

Lord Fallows, George was a banker by day, card fancier, and gambler by night, so he had to agree to marry Greta. But unfortunately, his family left him no choice as their family money was nearly gone, partly thanks to him.

George fancied himself a ladies' man. He was handsome, well-dressed, well-bred in the best schools, and had the right family name.

Greta had lots of money but only a little else. At 27, facing the alternative of spinsterhood and wanting children of her own, she agreed, of course, not knowing George's fondness for the 'gambler's' life.

The house itself took many staff to keep it clean and run well. Four floors in all. With the kitchen and servant's bedrooms below the stairs.

The first floor had a parlour, dining room, day room, and library, and the second floor held the ladies' bedroom, dressing room, and library for Lady Fallows. She insisted that the Ladies' parlour connecting to my room be turned into it as she read books that a 'gentlewoman' should not be seen reading.

Then, on the opposite side of the house were Lord's bedrooms, his dressing room, and a smoking room.

The second floor also held two guest rooms.

The third floor was the children's room, classroom/playroom and nanny's quarters, a bedroom, and a small sitting room of her own, where children's laughter could almost always be heard.

The staff members included the Cook, Mrs. Muller, known just as Cook. Lady Fallows insisted on a German cook, as she found English food bland and rather dull.

Nanny Jo (Johanna), Jon, Cook's 8-year-old son, attended to all the fireplaces, chickens, and kitchen garden and ran errands.

Two downstairs maids, Anne and Mary, and a butler named Albert. The Lady's maid and dresser, Liza. And the Lord's Valet, Mr. Smith.

The only meal Lady insisted they share to keep up appearances was breakfast, but of course, their staff was not slow-witted; they had known about the discourse in the house since the poor boy's birth and short life. That morning, Lord Fallows had quite a lot to say about their new living arrangements.

"How dare you? I'm the man of the house, not you," George's voice boomed, clearly asserting his perceived dominance. "Is it my fault my family has a name with no money? Is it my fault? No! Paid then to be forced to marry you, a foreigner? Significantly unpleasant to look at, woman! And your accent is so grading at the best times. How can I keep my head up and be the man of my house with your family holding the purse strings? My home, so what if it's bought with your inheritance? I'm still the man. Thank God, a woman can not own property; at least on paper, it's my house.

"Why was my family born to the title of a Lordship going back too many generations to count, with no land or money of note? To back it up?

"Oh, how I miss those school days, carefree, to be with any woman I wanted. No matter what class. Oh, how easily I could turn to a pretty face or the comely ankle of a dance hall girl.

"I worried about when my next allowance was due and how I should spend it," George's mind raced with the constant worry of financial dependence.

"Is it my fault I was not the scholar my parents wanted me to be? Or that I preferred wine, women, song, and gambling over my studies. Then what was my reward? What did they do to punish me? They married me off to you, a match they said was as good as the Queen's husband. But what did that matter? I was just a pawn in their game, a means to cover my debts and secure a job I despise. Marry me off to you!"

George's voice dripped with resentment, "They said German was no less a good match, like the Queen's husband. As though that would matter! Unless a direct descendant of the Crown, your family's money would cover my debts and get me a job.

"A job I must say, I hate! Just like doing penance. A banker of all things, having to count other people's money as a reminder that I have none of my own, and just like my school days, on a bloody allowance again.

"So all I have to keep me sane is gambling, cards, drinking at the club, and a few dolly mops. So, how did I know if one caused a disease?

"One less child in this world won't hurt, one less mouth to feed, one less brat for you to fawn over. It has given me a perfect way out. If I may be so bold, no more pretending I care for you or any of your brats. You, dear wife, have freed me from this suffocating life! You think it is a punishment for me never to share your bed again? No more sneaking in the front door, being quiet so as not to awaken anyone. You have given me a gift, not a punishment!"

"George, we have a farce of a marriage, but we must keep up appearances, including for the children and household staff. Everyone knows gossip travels fastest over the garden fence. We may not love each other, but we have a duty to our family and social standing.

"So I tell you to be here tonight for the children's play. They have been working so hard on their studies, including their German lessons, that they are almost fluent. This play is not just a performance; it's a testament to their dedication and a chance for them to shine. They are so proud and want to show you. The staff will also attend."

"I work hard, Greta, and I play cards on Wednesday nights. You planned this tonight to spite me!" Geroge snapped.

"Work hard? Do you work hard? It's your name alone that got you that job. With a request from *my* uncle, we would not live as we do without *my* money! You are best to remember that!" she retorted.

After dinner, George was a no-show.

"Mame, the children are getting restless. The Sir is over an hour late, and the youngsters are getting sleepy. Soon, it will be bath time."

"Please start, nanny. Without him, the children will be disappointed, but they still have the staff and me to watch tonight," Greta responded.

Life was good looking in from the outside, with family money and a job at the bank. It gave the Fallows' a very comfortable townhouse for a family of 6. The children had a nanny, a teacher, and six staff to keep the house clean and running as it should be.

Later that night, while the rest of the house was asleep, Greta was angry. So angry that George was not there for the children. It was striking midnight on the hall clock downstairs, and Greta was pacing in her room, muttering to herself, feeling disappointment, frustration, and a growing sense of simmering anger.

That man, how he makes me angry. Running with disgusting prostitutes but living large on my family's money! How I wish a woman could live independently. Raise her children, and even work at a job if she so chooses. But women do not have such a chance. It wouldn't be in my life if it were ever to change!

While the house was still silent, Greta decided to slip out and walk around to think about her plans. She found herself in the Whitechapel area, a rough part of the city.

She stood back in a doorway, looking at what was going on, when she spotted a prostitute. She was alone, no pub nearby, and it looked like she had had too much to drink.

Looking around some more, Greta noticed it was September, and the night air was warm enough that some were still walking around despite the late hour.

"Are you looking for company?" Greta asked, approaching the woman.

The woman looked at her up and down and said, "Why not? Women of your class need company, too; who am I to judge? Come along this way; I know a good spot for us not to be seen."

Following close behind, she spotted a wooden meat hammer and picked it up, hiding it in the folds of her skirt.

***

It's done. I can't believe I did it without being caught. I'm home now, but I still need to be very quiet. I clean up and return to my clothes before the staff wakes up.

I almost mess up the first time trying a mallet. I follow a lone woman into the ally, just at first to observe. But I end up being a witness to her wickedness. In a rage, I grab the wooden mallet from the gutter and go on the attack, not planning. It doesn't do the damage I want it to do. I only manage to knock her out. However, the anger is so intense that as I rage, I push the mallet quite a way up the opening of her woman's flower. The papers say her name was Emma Smith. She dies in due course from a wound I inflict.

Emma Smith

Getting the papers has become a guilty pleasure, but I can't let anyone see my glee; the reports are so far off the mark as to who the killer really is. So, I think I will continue to make them speculate. I believe those dolly mops and four penny knee benders, those women with no morals, have no idea how close to death they will be as long as I choose to rid the city of those loose women.

If I go to Whitechapel, I must fit in, so I am considering getting some well-used clothes. Something not so stylish as I will stand out in Whitechapel, but rather something older and warn out looking. So I go to the local church to donate my old clothes. I leave with an older, well-worn suit, stating it is for a masked ball.

It almost fits. The trousers are too short and worn well at the knees. The shirt is also too big, but I can roll the cuffs. The collar is shabby but fits well. To top it all off, I found this old houndstooth wool coat with some buttons missing. The hat I found is a little large. It is a cap style with a peak, but it works well to hide my hair, so it fits right.

I read somewhere that you shouldn't hunt near your home, so I will continue hunting in Whitechapel. It is an impoverished area of London with destitute people and poverty. With that comes prostitutes, pubs, and doss or rooming houses. And I've read that a few coins passing hands can satisfy illegal vices.

The following day, I tell staff that I am still unwell so that I can rest.

As I lay in my bed convalescing after the long and hard labour, bereaved at the loss of my poor wee boy. My heart and my breasts still ache for the boy who was born unable to live. All in thanks to that man, the family forced me to marry!

Once George is gone, I ask Jon, the houseboy, to bring me the day's papers. It will give my mind a break for a little while.

When a fascinating article catches my eye, I am always amazed at the difference between the news of the day and the fluff pieces they write for us women, "The Fairer Sex." My Lord, do they still think we have lesser intelligence because we are born as women?

Frederick Charrington uses a little-known criminal law, an amendment dated 1885, to rid the slum areas of known brothels operating out of doss houses. The article goes on to say that, 'All habitually unchaste women,' living in those east-end slums were able to earn more money on their backs in one night than in the sweatshops in an entire week.

These 'low-class prostitutes,' can be wives and daughters who turn out onto the streets for the livelihood of the unfortunate families living in what is called 'The evil quarter-mile, east, and west of Commercial Street' living in very low-class conditions.

In Carrington's campaign, the article says that any citizen can report a rooming house suspected of being a brothel to the police.

The trouble is that it backfires in a way, closing nearly 200 houses, which leads to the need to 'peddle their wares' in the streets and alehouses, no matter the weather, and at the mercies of all types of men. In some small ways, these ladies are safer in the brothels.

Reading this article shows me that men call the shots in every aspect of a woman's life. No matter what class you are born into, we all have our hardships and are at the mercy of men.

Reading the article for a second time and my blood is near-boiling. At the world's injustices toward women, I must live with the fact that I am forever bound to George.

Why are women, no matter what their birthright, but property to a man?

I am pacing now, trying to think of how I can get even with this. I have been dealt with because I am, "But a woman."

I am growing angrier, realising that the only way I may get free is if George is dead! Since, of course, divorce is not an option.

I must find a way to break free from George and reclaim my life. I refuse to be a victim of his vices. I must take action to ease the pain of losing my dear William, all because George enjoys the company of common prostitutes, loose women 'dolly mops,' 'two penny knee benders.'

His choices have put my life in jeopardy, and I fear I may never witness my children's milestones or experience the joy of their children. But I will not let him dictate the time I have left, which he stole from me by passing this low-class disease.

Like all the rest, I'm sitting in Whitechapel, in an alehouse, looking for a girl I can introduce my blade to. Only luck had Emma Smith's death on my count. This time, I will plan harder and get it just right.

There she goes around the room, seemingly known to all, as she sits with another street tramp, looking like they have been tossing back for quite a while tonight.

I shall sit in this dark corner sipping warm ale and watching what happens next.

By midnight, two girls leave together, each with a soldier on their arm. I think this night would be a waste, but I choose to wait a while longer; good luck (mine) and lousy luck (hers). My girl is alone again about 20 minutes later.

This time, she starts to wander away from the pubs, and toward the narrow lane I have noted before; George Yard has many small courts and alleyways.

Giving me plenty of opportunities to confront her and do my civic duty to rid London of all these diseased flesh peddlers.

"MURDER!" screams the morning papers again, and my body tingles at the thought of what they might have to say about me today. Maybe even a knife wound counts this time.

"George, did you see another murder last night? How terrible! I wonder if this will be all, or could there be more loose women being killed? Although I guess their choice of occupation does come with some danger." I mockingly say.

"Greta, it's not very nice for a woman of your place to get such interest in such a gruesome story; why can't you find better things to do with your time?" replies George.

"Like what, George, Drink? Gamble? Run with the wrong type of people, causing death and disease to your children? George, you have no right to criticise my choice of reading material." I reply.

"My family may not have the manners of a born lord or lady, but MY MONEY saved you and your family's good name from ruin. Of course, you like to let the world think otherwise, but we know the truth, don't we, George?" I firmly state.

I am nearly tingling with anticipation of what the papers are saying of last night's excursion; I barely heard all the awful things George was on about this morning. All I want is some time alone to pour over what the papers are saying and add it to my scrapbook.

Martha Tabram

The victim was named Martha. Two men spot her on the landing where I leave her, but only the second sounds the alarm; nearly morning, the dockworker notices the blood where the first man didn't bother to stop thinking that she was sleeping one off.

Later accounts state that the doctor who pronounced her dead had said at the time of autopsy that she was butchered thirty-nine times, seven into her lungs, and the possibly fatal stab was once through the heart. Wounds were later found in her throat, liver, spleen, and stomach. Such a force caused one to clear through her breastbone.

I find that my disguise is freeing. I can go places incognito without fearing meeting someone who knows me.

Tonight, I have a different plan. I shall steal away when the house is asleep to see what these opium dens are all about. I have heard much but need help understanding.

Who knows, maybe I'll look out for my next good-time sally and start as I constantly plot her untimely death. I'm finding the chase almost as much fun as the kill, and how else would I find out how the fairer sex works without a bit of exploration with my knife?

When I think I did the deed with Miss Emma Smith (the papers later told me), I have only knocked her out. The baton is not doing the deed I want; reading that she did not die right away and how she describes me, I dare say I need to laugh out loud with glee at how wrong she got it. I must remember to keep my head around the house.

The Opium Den

In the opium den, the room is large. However, the red and gold curtains and the many couches in candlelight make it feel small. The people, oh, the people, in all manner of dress or undress, men dressing as women, women as men, and sex was everywhere. No one seems to care who is there or watching—sitting, laying, twisting in the sheets. The most frightening of all is a man crouching in the corner. Who covered in sores, pulling his hair out in clumps all the while in a silent scream.

The smell was sickly, sweet, thick, and could have a scent making it so hard to catch one's breath. *How do those people take this smoke into their lungs? And for pleasure?* I see little comfort here. The smell is unlike anything I have ever smelt before, but it reminds me of country visits in my childhood.

The smell of a roof getting a new thatch, with the scent of near-burnt sugar and vanilla.

That is as close as I can come to describing the cloying, heavy smell of opium. The room spins, and I feel as if I may fall. I must leave and get out into the night air.

Running out of the door, I nearly fall into the street.

I need some clarification. *Which way do I go home?* I will not begin a hunt, for I know I will be making a fool's mistake. Instead, I leave home and plan for another day.

It's four on the clock, according to the town crier, and I hurry home, change back into my nightclothes, and slip into bed before the household starts to rise.

This night has frightened me, and I won't visit there again.

Sitting quietly reading the papers is a pleasure, especially when George does not grace us with his company. I think about how I shall hide my killing costume. Now that my disguise works well, I know that from the police and papers' descriptions. How easy it is for me to 'become a man.'

What shall I do, though, with my killing tools? How can I carry them without causing alarm? Using just the mallet was easy enough, hiding it in the coat.

Oh! The old bag, I had it when I moved to this awful city from my beautiful homeland here. Now, where is it? I know I saw it not long ago. In the children's play, Debbie carried some of her dolls in it. Now, that would be perfect. I must say.

I have some knives in the bag, which are helpful as needed and recently sharpened.

And finally, an old piece of nearly useless cloth to stuff in the woman's foul mouth so as not to be heard screaming.

I have grown fond of the mallet, my first instrument of destruction; I now use it to knock them about the head if they move too much while I cut them with my knife.

Hanbury Street as it was back then. Where Annie was found.

The man living at 29 Hanbury St. John Davis is the first to find the woman named Annie Chapman. Not seeing a police officer immediately, John tells several other men who decide to look at the body for themselves.

Anne Chapman

Finally, inspector J. Chandler of the H division on a nearby street follows John back to his yard.

Chandler looks over at Annie while waiting for more police to follow once the alarm sounds.

They are very shocked to see parts of Annie's intestines still connected to her insides but draped almost neatly over her right shoulder.

When the police surgeon shows up at 6:30 a.m., he finds more mutilations done at her killer's hands. The neck shows near strangulation and an attempt to cut her throat, nearly taking off her head.

Once at the morgue, The surgeon notes that the woman's whole uterus is removed. Dr. Phillips proposes that the murderer may have some medical knowledge and skill.

The next day, I'm sitting in my room, my mind racing in many directions. How easy it's getting, how close to being caught. The amount of fear and fascination the press is giving these killings.

And it's all for me, my work, something I am beginning to enjoy it if I am being candid about it.

The hunt is the choice of those so-called women. The thrill of the close calls while killing them. And the press, oh, the papers. I especially enjoy the speculations, for I am the one they fear.

How wrong they have it; that is the biggest thrill of all.

A person trying to claim my kills has written to the police and the papers to take credit for my work... leave it to a man to want to claim a woman's work. As in the literature of the day, a woman cannot write and get published unless it's under the guise of a man's name.

Oh, the wonder of a time and place where women have rights.

The only credit I shall give this one is the name he has given.

I am sure it strikes fear in the people's hearts.

A Hangover Room.

I shall claim this name, for I am Jack the Ripper.

At the next chance, I shall begin the hunt anew.

An Omnibus

Taking the omnibus to Whitechapel, I get off near the water pump and walk around. This part of the city is as busy at night as I expect it would be by day.

The smell of sewage is so strong as it runs in the street; there doesn't seem to be any proper plumbing down here except for the narrow gullies and gravity going downhill.

Another thing to note is the number of pubs and alehouses, almost one on every corner, none being very posh or festive, all dark, smelly, and crowded.

There, what's that? I hear a lady's voice, loud and much taken to her cups. I wander closer to the Frying Pan Ale House. Through the poorly cleaned windows covered with smoke and coal oil from the lamps, I look into the pub and spot her there, the one I choose to feel my blades next.

I walk a short distance to find a place to step out of sight of the street. To wait for my pry to leave. Little does this one know that she has but a few days left to live, so on the days I can get away from family, I follow her around to get a feel for her little part of Whitechapel and all the escape routes I may need to take.

In about three weeks, I will be ready for my next date. About 10 p.m. on her fateful night, I see that my girl is making the rounds of singing and flirting for pennies for a night of sleep at the doss house or, more than likely, more gin and, if lucky tonight enough for a hang-over room.

By midnight, two girls have left together, each with a soldier on their arm. I think this night will be a waste. But I choose to wait longer; good luck (mine) and lousy luck (hers). My girl is alone again about 20 minutes later. The hunt is still on! I follow up with her briefly and then approach her for a date. When I address her, I ask if she has a room, and I know she doesn't.

Learning in my travels to Whitechapel, "guests" are not permitted in the doss houses, and it is an immediate ban from the building if caught. "Follow me, my love; I know of a few private corners we could use."

"Lead the way, my lady."

Murder, murder, someone calls a constable; there's a dead woman here.

It is so quick, and I am nearly spotted before I can get away. Still, as luck is with me tonight, I spot a chimney sweeps ladder next to a building close by, climbing up to a flat roof and pulling the ladder up behind me; not only does it hide me and keep me safe, but I also have a front-row seat to the carnage I have created.

At about 3:45 a.m., she is found. The papers tell me the damage I have done.

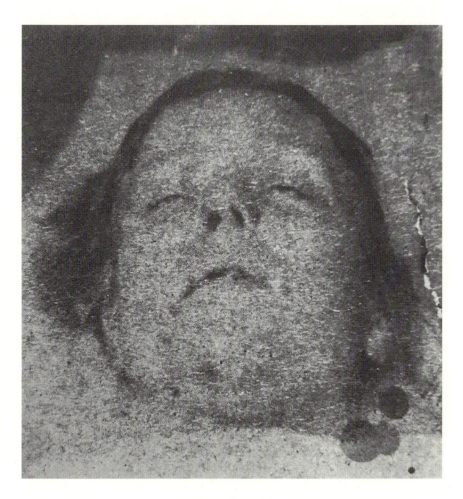

Mary Nichols

The woman was Mary Ann Nichols, not that it matters to me; a local doctor comes to the scene, and Mr. Henry Llewellyn is entirely forthcoming to the papers, seeming to enjoy going into details. We all like a bit of blood and gore with our morning coffee.

When the surgeon gets to the scene, he can feel parts of her body still warm. The police hold lanterns so the surgeon can look closer, and he finds two gashes across her throat. But her clothing, almost in place, reveals more wounds throughout her stomach and torso.

The most gruesome cut is from her slash, starting at her neck, about eight inches, and continuing down her spine.

Mr. Llewellyn speculates, "A long-bladed, moderately sharp knife must have caused the wound and used with great violence."

Several of the abdominal wounds are also very deep, and the murderer must have been facing Nichols, using one blade for all the injuries he inflicted.

Another breakfast, ignoring each other. Both of us are reading our newspapers.

You can nearly feel the tension as thick as a Christmas pudding.

"Greta! Must you read those? Have I not asked you before? What is your fascination with it?

"It would be best if you were reading your papers meant for women.

"Ladies Home Weekly or Gentlemen's Wife."

I sigh. "George, I may be your wife, but you, sir, are far from being a gentleman! Yes, my family's money gave you all this," I emphasise with a sweep of my arm, I then say, "You, as a man, claim it as your own, and as for Ladies Home weekly, how many times do I need a recipe for silver polish? How to arrange flowers to suit a room?"

"Some ladies would find it interesting, but George, I would rather know about This Edison fellow's light bulb or Mr. Bell's Telephone."

"I don't understand you, Greta. Why can't you be content with your role as my wife and mother?" He roars as he slams his fist hard enough to shake the glasses on the table before him.

"Because George, I loathe you. And if times were different, you would not have my money to throw away on your gambling and loose women. I would divorce you in an instant, and you would be left destitute." I say to George.

"Well, Greta, the feeling is mutual, but even though I could divorce you, I am trapped because I need your money to live the life I am accustomed to, and I deserve it!

"If you were even a little appealing to me, those loose women you speak of would not be necessary," George replies.

"Enough George! I will not be spoken to like that in my own house! And do not even try blaming me for your dirty little habit!

"I do not have any blame for that!"

"Good day, Greta. Another pleasant breakfast to send me off to a job I hate. Don't wait for dinner for me; I have a card game I must attend tonight."

Alone, at last, that awful man is gone. I can read the papers at leisure now. I leave out a long sigh as I sit down again.

The police blotter still has no idea who the killer is, so they are wrong in where they are looking.

I have even bought two copies, one to save in a secret scrapbook I have been compiling, which is well hidden that I may take out in leisure when alone.

The Séance

Here is something of mild interest, A seance; they are all the rage. I wonder if they are authentic. There is something after this life; there has to be more than this.

Okay, here is an exciting announcement: Elizabeth Murry will have one at her house. I would like to know if I can get an invitation to join her, although we have met at different functions and we have never really been friends. I'll send a note, and maybe I could join in. It could prove educational.

Later in the day, I sit in my library and pen a note.

"Johnny, see this note delivered to Elizabeth Murry. She lives over on 10 Cross Street, do you know it?"

"Yes, Mame, two streets down and one over the red door?" "Yes, that's it. Wait for a reply."

"Here, Mrs. I returned as quick as I could. Mrs. Murry took her time to write a reply."

The Note:

My Dearest Greta,

I was pleased and a little surprised to receive your note.

It has been a while since we saw each other, as you tend to keep to yourself.

I hope your family is well and you have recovered from losing your last child. It's terrible for any woman to lose a child after carrying it to full term.

I am hosting one on the seance next week, Thursday Eve.

The medium insists on only eight at a table sitting at most, and we were full, But as luck would have it, one of my guests could not attend as expected, so,

Yes, you may come and be amazed. We plan to connect to those poor, unfortunate women of Whitechapel.

To see if they may be able to identify their Murderer.

Until then, I remain,

Your friend Elizabeth.

Smiling as I put down the note, I start thinking, *Interesting, should I be concerned? Is that person an authentic medium and could converse with the dead? What will happen? Can those dolly mops tell the living who I am?*

No, I need not worry. I am careful to disguise myself and always behind the trollops when I strike the first blow. I'll be fine. This will prove to be an exciting evening, as I love to learn new things.

When Thursday arrives, I do my best to dress carefully, looking my best in a lady-like fashion, which can be difficult for me, given my German background and today's styles.

As people gather at Elizbeth's house, she sets a large round table with chairs in her parlour. Elizabeth is excitedly greeting her guests and anxious to get started.

"Most of you already know each other, so I won't make those introductions. But I am honoured to introduce you to world-renowned author Sir Arthur Conan Doyle! Like all of us, he is very interested in the other side's world and what we here may learn tonight with the help of the world-famous James Stanton Moses.

"James has been known not only in England but also in parts of Europe. He has also been invited to the Colonies next year when the weather clears enough to sail.

"Oh, and here he is now. So I'll let him explain how tonight will go."

"Good evening, all. I'll have you all sit at the table, where we will hold hands throughout the scene. It is imperative that you do not break contact with each other, or we will lose the connection to the spirit. Therefore, I have asked that only one large candle be placed in the centre of the table and just a few others scattered sparingly around the room.

"Our Gracious hostess has asked that we try to contact the tragically departed ladies of Whitechapel, and because there are more than one, we will concentrate on those for tonight."

While listening to this man, I am becoming a little nervous. My hands are getting damp, and I fear they will give me away when it is time to join hands. So, looking like I am smoothing the rough silk of my mauve dress, I dry them there.

As bad luck has it, I am sitting between the medium and Sir Doyle, wondering if I should have risked coming.

"Please let me explain what may happen," James continues; "The table may rock, move, or even tip. The Departed guest may rap on the table. I have devised once for yes, twice for no. So, if we ask questions, keep them simple, such as yes or no answers.

"I sometimes go into a trance-like state, and it may appear like I am asleep. The departed will choose me to speak directly to all of you. This method is something I am only aware of because people tell me this has happened. I have no memories of this type of communication. We can begin by dimming the light, all but those I indicated. Please join hands now; remember, do not break hands, as it will cut off the connection to the other side.

"We are here to contact the unfortunate ladies of the Whitechapel murders and ask you to come forward to help us shed light on who cut your lives short in such a horrible manner. Please step closer to the veil between our worlds and help us find your killer."

Suddenly, the table seems to tremble, and I feel something brush my foot! *Don't move.* I stayed still, afraid to move any part of my body to investigate. I was holding my breath. *It will pass, and don't dare let them know you are frightened by your expression.* Nothing, I'm sure it was nothing that touched my foot.

James began to speak: "Maryann, Annie, Catherine? Are you near? Can you move closer? Let us know your life's end moments. Are you able to describe your killer? Or killers? Please give us a sign."

Moments pass, and the ticking of the hallway clock seems louder as time passes. Around the table, people are starting to fidget the longer they wait. Finally, Sir Doyle clears his throat, "Come on, man, nothing is happening."

"Give us a few more minutes, please. I'm sure they are close by, but they feel, yes, I think they are still confused, not understanding that they have passed because it was so sudden, so violent."

Just then, the table trembles harder—no mistake on that. Then, a window flies open seemingly on its own, and because of that, most of the room's candles go out. With that, James whispers loudly, "Be still. There is someone here. I will see if they can communicate with us.

"Are you one of the unfortunate ladies who recently lost their lives?

"(Nothing) If you are, can you knock once? I am aware it will be difficult for you."

"Still nothing! My God, man, are you trying to fool us intentionally?

"Less than nothing is happening," says Sir Doyle.

James took a long breath and said, "Sometimes, the spirit chooses not to come forward for many reasons. They may not know that they are dead yet and are confused. They may like where they are now and don't want to return for many other reasons.

"In tonight's case, I'm afraid no connection was made.

"I must conclude tonight. Please do not think this is the usual outcome, as I usually have great success, and contact me again for your seance."

"Not bloody likely! Why throw good money away? You could throw it in the Thames River for all the good you do. You, sir, are a fake and a charlatan! I will make it my mission to let all the good people know not to use you! My scepticism is at its peak, and I can't help but voice my doubts."

"Please, Mr Doyle, you will kill my livelihood and close many doors for those who wish to communicate with loved ones on the other side."

As this heated debate continues, I decide it is a good time to leave after a brief goodbye to the hostess.

It is such a relief. My crimes are still safely hidden, and I sit back with a sigh in the handsome cab ride home.

Enjoying the morning as usual, George is not home to pretend to be social for the sake of our children and, of course, the gossipy house staff. I take my tea in the parlour, the morning light filtering through the lace curtains, casting a delicate pattern on the floor. It's a peaceful moment, a brief respite from the chaos I've unleashed, which I find strangely delightful.

I can sit longer with my morning tea, reading the press on my murders, not only in the legitimate papers but the broadsides and pamphlets of the day. Oh, how I secretly enjoy those little papers that are, let's face it, made for people who have little or no education. The drawings alone are worth every one or half pence it costs me.

My actions have caused quite a stir in Whitechapel. It's a strange feeling, knowing that people are coming together in response to my deeds, taking the lead where they think the police are falling behind. There's a mix of pride and guilt that I can't quite shake off, but there's also a strange sense of accomplishment in the chaos I've unleashed, a feeling I can't help but savour.

Samuel Montaque, the Parliament member for the area, offers a one hundred pound reward for my capture. But sadly, the home office will not let police print or distribute flyers with the said reward.

Another group of local business owners try to form 'The Miles End Vigilance Committee' in Whitechapel, but they are also turned down. This same committee then writes to Her Majesty the Queen, and the group is again refused any help from the government. It's both a relief and a burden to see these efforts fail. Relief that I remain free, but a burden of guilt, knowing that these people are suffering because of me.

Failing that, another group takes a different approach. 'St. Jude's District' tries to put people on the street between 11 p.m. and 1 a.m., watching for suspicious activities and then both inform and help the police if need be.

Suspense and fear run high in Whitechapel, usually a busy place after dark. It is almost empty after midnight, and some streetwalkers move to other areas or refuse to come outside.

I am both ashamed and impressed at what I am doing for the people of London right now. If they only knew that a mere woman was the cause of all this fear. It's a constant battle within me, the conflict between my actions and my conscience. I am torn, but I cannot turn back now. My work still needs to be done. My knives will sing again.

Life at home needs my attention, so some time goes by as time usually does when the morning papers announce:

Suspicions and fear run high after the last one called Annie in the papers. Whitechapel, usually busy, is almost empty after midnight. Some known prostitutes move to other parts of London or refuse to come outside for fear of their own lives.

So, I have all of London at my feet and in the grip of fear for my actions. Oh, how I wish I could openly claim it.

A mob has gathered outside the police station, shouting and being an all-around total nuisance of themselves, crying for vengeance.

I nearly drop my teacup when I read this: vengeance for a trollop, who none cared for when she lived spreading disease.

NOW they care! Then, in the quiet times between murders, all of London is afraid. Two women attacked in the west end, and the papers report that they are my handy work. Annie is at the forefront of the news with the inquest.

I am wrong in thinking I can take a break. It seems I must hunt again as people are now reporting to be less afraid and roaming free of fear; it appears in Whitechapel. With the lack of credible news about me, although the papers are wild with fabrications and questions left unanswered.

I decide I must hunt again because a hunt is what it has become: a mission. These women are barely human and deserve to be put down like the animals they have become. Spreading their diseased legs for anyone with a hay penny or more!

I spot a woman leaving a doss house and take this opportunity to follow her. Of course, she enters a murky old pub like all the other pubs in Whitechapel. I will wait it out for a bit to see if she comes out soon. The wait is short, and she comes outside.

But a well-dressed man approaches her as I am about to step out of the shadows. I see the conversation exchanged, although not close enough to hear. The two move further down the street, and he tries to kiss her. I have to walk away in disgust; kissing is such an intimate thing to do; one should only be done between adults in a romantic relationship. Even though I have been married all these years, bearing his children, I could never accept or exchange a kiss like that with George. However, lying with him in our marital bed was not so bad because I could close my eyes and transport myself back to my childhood home in Germany. I play with those happy memories as if I were again there and not engaging in my marital duties. I only agreed to it because it was expected, and of course, I wanted my children.

Back from that memory, still in Whitechapel. I watch this woman because she will be next to feel my knives' cold, hard steel. It is as if my blades sing and want to be free again. So, I wait and watch, but as I attempt to leave the shadows, a second man approaches, well dressed, with a hat very similar to mine but in the current style, different from the older type of the one I wear myself. This man engages in a short conversation, but my prey shakes her head, looking as if she is about to turn him down.

But this man is cunning, pulls a red flower out of his coat, and hands it to her. She laughs, smiles and accepts it. Then, taking this man's arm, they walk toward the darkened streets; all the while, she fastens it to the buttonhole in her coat.

What to do? I know those whores have tricks, the ability to finish a man quickly; for most, it is done outdoors in the streets and darkened alleyways. So again, I choose to wait, and I will decide if she will be done tonight or soon enough. This dollymop is the next one I want.

Elizabeth Stride

Just as I think this low woman is a pro, she takes this man not too far away and finishes him quickly with her tricks.

I wait until the well-dressed man passes me, and I go in for the kill.

She has her back to me. Arm outstretched, leaning on a fence, she seems to be whipping herself down with a rag. I step up quickly and quietly drag my blade across her neck, but before I can do my work,

I hear a pony cart turn into the alleyway about a block away, so I gather my tools and run. The papers tell all the damage that I have done.

I nearly sever the windpipe entirely in two, and blood is running down in the gutter into the drain, still warm when touched.

This incision is so deep that Stride's head is barely attached to her body. As a result, her head is nearly removed from her body.

As I run from the body, going away from the approaching cart, I can't help feeling cheated and unsatisfied at the last kill, unable to display her as she deserves to be. However, my luck is with me. As I turn a corner in a nearby lane, another whore is throwing up in the gutter. Again, thank you, Providence. She is put right in place. I take advantage and pull out a long knife, again catching her from behind. I run my blade across her neck, and she goes down quickly.

Looking about, I start my mutilation quickly before I can be interrupted again.

Running my large blade down her torso, I reach in and pull out some of her insides, working quickly because I am close enough to my last victim that the whistles and shouting of the police running around are too close for my comfort. I barely remember what I have done to her, but I quickly pack my tools and run off toward the main street and the omnibus home.

On this last trip to Whitechapel, I find a loose woman with a room of her own, which I find interesting. So, I pay close attention to her routines and the streets around her room. In planning, I discover that her space is shared with another. They have worked out a system for who uses the room and when.

And even a small stack of stones nearby signals that the room is in use. I also find that a windowpane is broken, but I can reach through and unlock the door. I retreat and plan for another day.

George graces me with his presence at breakfast the next day, in body anyway.

"George, where have you been? You have not been home in the last three nights; the children have noticed and are asking questions I don't know how to answer."

"Now here you are, turned up again like a bad penny."

"Greta, my dear," he answers with a sneer. "Unfortunately, as you often tell me, I have no home to call my own."

"So I have secured lodgings at my club when the hour grows too late to return home. So you have taken to bolting the doors at eleven of the clock. I'm more welcome there than in my own home."

Right, I think, probably at a whore house more likely, must I take to following my husband? This may be the best time to think of stopping my killing spree. I'm growing tired of all this anyway, and the longer I go on, the more chances I have of getting caught.

But how to end it?

Later that same day, while the household staff are busy and the children are out with their nanny, I return to my library and take out my special scrapbook, plus the full uncut papers with any mention of my Whitechapel murders. Going through the pages, I am proud of my time in Whitechapel.

I am aware of my kill clothing, knives, and the leather apron I find on one of my hunts, which are well hidden behind the boiler in the basement.

One last girl, I think to myself. I will make it extra gruesome, and the woman with the room shall be perfect. I can take my time without fear of being seen.

This time, I will bring old clothes that belong to George so I can get them covered in her blood, as I have thought of a way to get rid of him. But I need a night he chooses to be at home for it to work.

Three nights later, George is home; after having yet another fight, he retreats to his study. I wait a bit, and as any good wife would do, I fix him a drink as an apology, but with a sleeping tonic in it to be sure he wouldn't choose to go out after he thinks I am asleep.

So, the end begins. I dress warmly because the winter weather is approaching. My killing tools and George's clothes are tucked neatly inside my carpetbag.

I return to the small street where the girl has her room, and I wait. The wait is not long, but she has company, so I retreat to a doorway nearby to be out of the cold wind and prying eyes; the man is done and leaves shortly, and I see through her tattered curtain, so old it is nearly just a tattered rag with no colour of note. Before she wakes up, I slit her throat and start doing my work in peace.

I first remove my topcoat, carefully putting it far enough away to not get blood on it. And on a small side table, I take out my knives. I look around the tiny room as I do, and it is not much bigger than our coal room at home, with a small bed that is hardly big enough for one adult, lumpy straws poking out everywhere, and I swear even in this poor light I can see bugs jumping in and out and around the mattress.

I take a chance to light the stub of a candle and place it on the floor so it may not be from the outside and set to work.

Angry, and yes, even in a frenzy, I do more damage to this one than all the others. Maybe it is my rage over what my life has become or taking advantage of the perfect kill sight, but by the amount of time I feel I have spent. Even I, am in horror at what I have done.

Her body is lying open like a gutted fish. I remove both breasts, parts of her face, internal organs, heart, and other things, which I have spread around her and in the room for those who find her to see what she had become.

Then, I remove George's clothes, drawing them through the blood. The shirt and pants are a good set with the tailor's mark still attached, so its owner will not be mistaken. It was soon dawn, and I can see the sun just over the taller buildings. I must leave before I am seen here in Whitechapel or missed at home.

Over the next few days, I put together a box of things from each kill, including the apron, with a piece of leather taken out and even my knives; oh, how I will miss them. I include some news articles and broadsheets, reluctantly giving up some of my souvenirs.

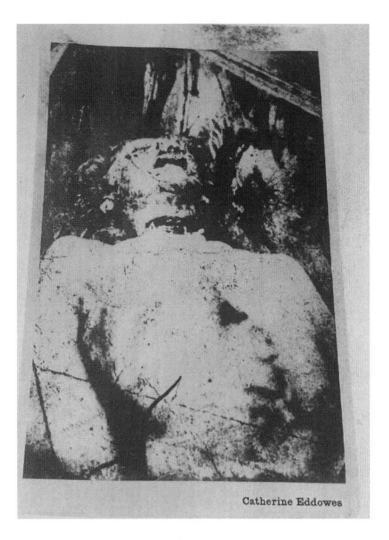

Catherine Eddowes

After the news of my final kill got out, my unfortunate "friend" was named Catherine Eddowes, according to the papers. I go through the box again, adding the heart; after cooking it because it is beginning to smell funny, I don't remember taking it out, let alone bringing it back with me. Then, ensuring all was in place, especially the bloody clothing, I close George's box and leave it in nearly plain sight with a satisfying bang.

Two days later, I feel that the box is too well hidden in cold storage for the staff to find, So I decide we need Jam for our afternoon tea and go to the cold storage myself to find the box.

I ensure the kitchen staff are on hand when I bring the box into the kitchen's light. When opening, we all are shocked and disgusted at my well-thought-out contents.

"Jonny, go and fetch the nearest constable at once. Please don't stop looking until you have found one and bring him home." Soon, the house is overrun with police, a doctor, the coroner, and other people to know who all the others were.

The parlour is used to question family and staff, although I refuse to interview the children. Police have long since taken the box away and ask where George is and when he is expected home.

This is my time to shine (I should be on stage), crying and "breaking confidences" about our lives since finding out about his lifestyle after our last child's unfortunate birth and death.

The staff stays close and supportive, agreeing with me on more things than they know. Finally, the police agree it is time to pick up George for questioning.

Not finding him at his bank, police are dispatched to his club. It is quite the show, with many police swarming the building, running room to room looking for George.

Of course, once found, George is mainly drunk and then very confused about what the police are talking about and what they have to do with him. In short, he is arrested and put in the back of a police wagon.

The crowd outside, having gathered, somehow manages to find rotten food and throw it at George and the wagon as it goes past on the street toward Commercial Street Station in Shoreditch, as it is where most of the work on the Whitechapel murders was centred.

Getting George to see straight takes several pots of strong black coffee. Many people handle the box, and the Chief of Police soon decides that no one else should touch it and its contents. Photographing and numbering each item, he locks it in his office except for the piece of cooked meat that is beginning to smell and is dispatched to the coroner, who is tasked with identifying it.

Detective Fredrick George Abberline, who took the lead in most Whitechapel murders, spends nearly sixteen hours questioning a perplexed George. At the same time, police further searches the house and stables. I am very pleased with myself for having the forethought of hiding all of my killing costumes and the treasured scrapbook. But, knowing full well, I'll need to dispose of the clothes very shortly.

All the while, George is close to being tortured and given very little food, drink and sleep. News boys are already crying. Scotland Yard finally catches the Whitechapel killer. Newspapers, broadsheets, pamphlets, and even penny dreadfuls are already screaming gory details as they come out, whether it is the fact or not, anything to make a sale.

It only takes five days for Judge Sir James Alexander Glencross to fill a grand jury. But first, 17 men are found suitable, and then, the trial decides to move to Old Bailey courts, giving the magnitude and momentum the prosecution will have. Then, to prepare testimony for a ridiculously short trial, with the help of the press and, of course, my box of souvenirs.

Crowds continue to grow around the courthouse, with people from all over London and further afield. Streets are taking on a carnival atmosphere with peddlers and food vendors.

People crowd the ale houses so much that owners sell spirits in the street. No bed can be found for any amount of money, so people sleep on the roads and alleyways nearby in make-shift camps and around small fires after dark.

The Trial

The trial begins on a very wet and gloomy Monday morning. As a dutiful wife, I take it upon myself to hire an incompetent counsellor, barely out of law school and looking like a frightened rabbit about him. Donald Rowlandson asks me why I choose him. I confide that although appearances look otherwise, George has gambled most of our money away, and I am concerned if I can even pay him in full if the trial becomes lengthy. (But this is a lie, of course)

The young Barrister seems satisfied with that answer. Of course, I plan on being in the courthouse every hour that the trial will take and being available to testify if needed, which I am only too happy to do, "If only to clear my husband's good name," from all these terrible accusations.

The trial is swift, with people nearly coming to blows to get a seat in the courtroom.

Judge Sir Glencross decides that a town crier can go outside twice daily to tell the crowd what is happening inside.

One by one, the murdered women are brought up in order of the dates killed, time found, and by who. Then, Tomas Walker, the coroner, will go over the wounds' photographs, police testimonies, and crime scene photos.

Barrister Henry Smith, for the Crown, asks that I am not used as a character witness, stating spousal privilege; the court calls both housemaids and the cook. They all paint a bleak picture of our marriage, especially after the death of baby William, and I am right; it is tough to hide secrets from household staff.

All three repeat a nasty picture of George, his gambling, and the many arguments we have about the company he likes to keep. How right after the death of the newborn, I locked him out of my bedroom for good. All the while, I was being nice to him in front of the other children and staff.

It takes all I can not to smile at the whole thing, even needing to hide behind my handkerchief to suppress the little smile I have when they each finish their testimony.

Young Mr. Rowlandson chooses not to allow George to testify, feeling it will do more harm than good.

Mr Smith asks the judge if the jury can have a tour of Whitechapel and the five kill sites, as none of the jurors have ever set foot on that side of London, and after a feeble attempt to stop it from Rowlandson, the request is granted. The judge's clerk arranges an omnibus for the next day.

One would have thought a parade was coming through town. The judge, two barristers, the Chief of Police, the coroner, and the seventeen men on the jury board the omnibus with a sizable crowd of people not wanting to miss a moment of action, all following closely behind on the way to Whitechapel. With George locking up tight at the station, the judge directs me not to come, as it is unsuitable for a lady of my standing.

I give all staff the day off and instruct the nanny to take the children out for a picnic, stating that I need time away from everyone and all that is happening. When I am sure I am alone, I fire up the kitchen stove and burn my killing costume.

The day after, the jury and all have their tour. Finally, the trial ends, and the jury heads to a back room to decide George's fate. Only to return a mere four hours later with the guilty verdict on all five counts of aggravated assault and murder.

Judge Glencross comments on how quickly the jury returned with the verdict, and the head juror states, "Oh, we were done in less than one hour but decided we would share one last lunch paid for by the city's own pockets." At which the court erupts into laughter.

The judge rapped his gavel to quiet the room and stated, "There is no need to prolong sentencing. We will return here tomorrow."

The next day, the courtroom is again bursting with people here to have first-hand knowledge of George's fate. The room fell to a quiet whispering, then silent, ready to hear what was in store for George.

"Lord George Fallows, please stand to receive your punishment." While standing, George tries to speak, "But, your honour," Glencross repeats again.

Going to the Gallows

"The time for denial is over. You have been found in a court of law by a jury of your equals, guilty of five counts of aggravated assault and murder, and in finding this decision, I sentence that you will be hung by your neck until dead three days from now because that is how long it takes to build gallows in the square outside this same courthouse.

"May God show you more mercy than the mercy you showed those poor unfortunate women.

"This trial is over. Please remove the prisoner."

As George passes me, I let him see the fleeting smile on my face before quickly covering it up with my handkerchief and faking a great sob. Concerned people and well-wishers immediately surrounded me.

On the day of execution, I do not attend, nor do I allow any of my staff. Instead, we dress the house in black crepe, with mirrors draped, and have mourning wreaths on all windows and doors facing the streets. I instruct staff that I will not be accepting guests of any kind in the foreseeable future.

I am spending all my time with my children. Days, then weeks, go by, and slowly, the Whitechapel murders are no longer in the papers or on the minds of most Londoners.

I still have my scrapbook and continue adding to every news article and broadsheet that mentions the murders, trials, and executions.

Seasons change as they tend to, and I am happy and free for the first time. With everyday life returning to a new normal, George's estate is settled, and I make a point of paying his gambling debts.

Since my family's money bought nearly everything but his title, everything has been returned to me through an uncle who is too old to care what I want or what I plan to do with it.

It is easy to sell off our London home, except for some key pieces of furniture, clothing and toys for the children, and of course, I get to keep my beloved library.

We all return to my native Germany, buying a small acreage with an excellent house. Having everything as a London house but on a smaller scale. I also invite all of the London houses' staff as they know how I like things and are loyal to me. As such, there is a substantial raise in their pay to relocate. Now that I'm a widow, free from answering to any man, I can use my money as I wish.

The children are growing, all well-educated and excited for life. My health isn't what it should be, and I may not live to see the youngest grow into a fine young man. The one bright spot, however, is that my children have titles, many opportunities that will come their way, and my family's money.

I am saddened that I may never get told to hold a grandchild because of George's unhealthy lust. I have made arrangements for each of the children should my life end too soon.

As for today, I sit under a large willow tree in my meadow, watching the nanny and the children play close to the nearby pond. I flip through a large leather-bound book that holds my secret with a sturdy lock on it, and the key I wear around my neck and its contents are for my eyes only.

The End

Who was Jack the Ripper?

There are so many speculations on who Jack was. They even have a name for people, and I guess I am one also;

Ripperologist

Ripperology—**A sometimes obsessive interest in studying the crimes of Jack the Ripper**— fascination for more than 100 years to his gruesome crimes and the fact he was never caught.

The shawl of Catherine Eddowes, miraculously surviving all these years, is a testament to the enduring mystery of Jack the Ripper.

In March 2019, DNA data was collected at the University of Leads in the UK through a new genetic analysis by Dr Jari Louhejainen and Dr David Miller. This groundbreaking research was then published in the Journal of Forensic Sciences.

Mitochondrial (Mother's) DNA

Catherine's blood is taken, and they then match the semen to a descendant of a person of interest at the time. Jack was proven to be Aaron Kosminski, a 23-year-old barber from Hastings, London, originally from Poland. It can be noted he was one of many prime suspects at the time.

Then, in 2024, using the same shawl but newer, more refined techniques, the contamination of over 100 plus years and a question of whether Catherine owned it. The provenance or proof of original ownership.

Renewed questions start again, and critics question if the 2019 results are correct, leaving myself and countless others still very much invested over any new bits of information. But as of this writing, our Jack is still a mystery.

Bibliography

Although this is a work of fiction, I have been fascinated with Jack since I first read of him in middle school. I think I have read every book, fiction and non-fiction and seen every movie and documentary out there.

These are the ones I used to help me write my story using the historical timeline:

A&E's History magazine Jack the Ripper: The World's Most Notorious Cold Case

Published by Time Inc. Books

11/16/2018

Jack The Ripper CSI Whitechapel

Paul Begg and John Bennett

Illustrated by Jaakko Luukanen

Published 2012 Carlton Publishing Group London

The Jack The Ripper Files, Illustrated History Of The Whitechapel Murders

Richard Jones

Published 2015 Carlton Publishing Group London

The Invention Of Murder, How The Victorians Revealed In Death

And Detection And Created Modern Crime.

Judith Flanders

Published 2011 HarperCollins Hammersmith London

The Victorians

A.N.Wilson Arrow Books

Published 2003

Plus, Google and Wikipedia

I have also used many photos and information from multiple sources, adding to the Fictitious storyline as it follows the actual case in the Summer and Fall of 1888.

Dictionary and Thesaurus

Because this happened in 1888 England, I used actual, old English terms in some places to help the story move along. You will find all of them here; if not, there is everybody's old friend, Google.

Laudanum

Possibly one of the most well-known Victorian medicines. It was a cocktail of opium alkaloids, including morphine and codeine, combined with alcohol. Although there was no single formulation for laudanum, it typically contained approximately 10% Opium combined with up to 50% alcohol. It was highly addictive. Due to its bitter taste, it could be mixed with many things, including spices, honey, ether or chloroform, wine, whiskey or brandy, and even mercury or hashish. Depending on the strength of the tincture and the severity of symptoms, a typical adult dose ranged from ten to thirty drops.

Opium

Opium was legal in Britain in the early 1800s, with people consuming between 10 and 20 tons of the stuff every year. Powdered Opium was dissolved in alcohol as a tincture called laudanum, which was freely available as a painkiller and even present in cough medicine for babies. We are well aware of the dangers and addictions of Opium today, but it was a widely used "cure-all" back then.

Syphilis

By the late 18th century, a staggering one in five Londoners had contracted syphilis by the age of 35, a shocking testament to the widespread health issues of the time.

This disease was not confined to a particular social stratum, affecting both men on the fringes of the city's economy and wealthy individuals involved in London's sex trade, underscoring its far-reaching impact.

People with syphilis could infect their wives and children, who could be born with risk factors.

Syphilis inflicted its victims with a range of painful and repulsive symptoms, including inflamed skin with scabs, swellings, and tubercules, painting a vivid picture of the suffering endured.

Omnibus

The typical London omnibus was an enclosed and glazed carriage with four wheels drawn by one or two horses. Passengers could sit on benches to either side inside, enter via a door at the rear, or climb up to exposed seats on the roof. A driver would ride at the front of the carriage, with a <u>conductor</u> assisting passengers to climb aboard or depart and taking fares at the rear.

Broadsheet

The genesis of the broadsheet newspaper can be traced back to 18th-century Britain. Although the reasons aren't obvious, the British government placed taxes on newspapers relating to their number of pages. To still sell papers, publishers made their products much larger to decrease page count despite the new versions being more challenging to hold.

Penny Dreadful

The 'penny dreadful' has been described as a "19th-century phenomenon" which took the art of publishing by storm. A 'penny dreadful' was a story published in pamphlets piece by piece each week, costing only a penny. They're also known as penny blood, penny awful, and penny horrible. All in all, pretty dreadful!

Due to the improvement of education and literacy skills in the 1800s, the penny dreadful became increasingly popular. Typical penny dreadfuls had stories of monsters, mysteries, and the supernatural.

Pamphlet

An unbound book (that is, without a hard cover or binding). Pamphlets may consist of a single sheet of paper printed on both sides and folded in half.

Sleeping Tonic

Alcohol (gin for the poor and whisky or brandy for the wealthier) or the readily available Opium in one form or another, with the most popular being laudanum, a tincture of alcohol and morphine. It was unrestricted, and anyone could buy it almost anywhere.

Victorian Morning Practices

For women during the Victorian period, mourning attire included every conceivable article of clothing, hair accessories, stationery, umbrellas, fans, and purses. The material most associated with mourning was black silk crepe, which had a flat, lifeless quality.

Widows were expected to mourn for two years and were allowed to wear grey and lavender only in the last six months of 'half-mourning.' Children in middle-class Victorian families were required to wear full black mourning clothes for one year after the death of a parent or sibling. Girls dressed very much like their mother's dress.

Some mourning superstitions

- Curtains were closed, and servants covered all the mirrors until after the funeral so the deceased's image wouldn't get trapped in a looking glass.
- It was thought that you might be next if you saw yourself in a mirror at a house where someone had recently died.
- All the clocks were stopped at death to prevent bad luck.
- And somewhat creepily, Victorians turned family photographs face-down to protect family and friends from possession by a spirit of the dead.

The wreath let community members know that there had been a death in the household. The customs of the time, even the colour of the ribbon, would tell what family member and even child sex.

So, people who passed by quietly and out of respect, even children, were taught to play on a different street out of earshot of a home with a wreath on the door.

Most funeral wreaths were made up of black ribbons or black crepe.

The house may also be draped in mourning cloth if affored, much like we string lights in our windows at Christmas today.

Dictionary and Glossary of terms

Doss House

In the UK, a Doss house was a place for people to stay for very little money; it was men, women, and even families who couldn't afford regular housing. There was a shared Outhouse, no separation of sexes or ages, and most didn't even have any way of cooking meals.

Sit-ups

For a penny, a homeless person could pay to 'sit up' on a bench all night in a hall. This was sometimes the only option for people to get off the streets, especially in England's wet and freezing winters. The only downside to these arrangements was that they weren't supposed to sleep in these 'sit-ups.' Some places even hired monitors to ensure no one fell asleep because, for a penny, you are paying to sit indoors and not fall asleep.

Two - penny Hangover

Although safer than the streets, most were still associated with being. Poor England could pay to sleep sitting up and hanging over a ship's rope, the longest length of a tenement room. Then, the rope would be released every morning at about five or six am, and you were sent on your way.

Finally, for the most luxurious

A bed in London's poor side of town, you could sleep in a coffin bed for 4p a night, have a tarpaulin (ship oilcloth covering) for warmth, and even have a meal in the morning. Note of interest: these houses were the original Salvation Army men's shelters.

Dollymop/Strumpet

A woman who is sometimes a prostitute.

Usually, they are very young and sent out to do this to help the family.

Four Penny Kneebender

A man or woman who will give you oral sex for 4 pennies, usually not an actual prostitute but desperate for money.

The Victorian class systems

The class system in 1800s England was so different from what we know today.

Upper class

Royalty Nobility (Lords, Ladies, Dukes, Duchesses)

Usually worked for their wealth but inherited it down the bloodline. Having land and more extensive estates (Castles even), Lords and Dukes had the privilege of sitting in parliament and making laws. However, being upper class sometimes meant they were out of touch and not qualified to make those laws and regulations.

The Upper class was divided further of note:

***Royals:** made up of just Royal families

***Middle-upper class**: Officers and Lords

***Lower-upper Class**

Made up of "self-made wealthy men and successful business owners." This class lived in larger houses and employed one or two people to help run their homes, such as a cook or a maid.

The working poor

Lived in tiny, overcrowded, cold, damp homes and shared an outside toilet with neighbours. Very few would be dwellings as we know them today, but instead, they live in tiny apartments with no kitchen to cook hot meals in, although some may have a room with a cooking fire shared by all those living there.

Finally, the destitute class.

These were people who did not have work or had so little money they could not pay to be considered working poor; sadly, it was usually women and children who no longer had husbands or fathers. Or the breadwinner was injured on the job and could not work. They are the ones who used the Doss houses and the likes if they were able to come up with the pennies needed. Many women with their children or single refused to use those because of the danger they would be in. So chose to live in the streets and doorways of Victorian England.

Made in the USA
Columbia, SC
01 May 2025